W9-BFW-592

DISCARD

Froggy went a-Courtin'

SMITHSONIAN INSTITUTION

To Graham, builder of houses for frogs and mice—J.D.

Book copyright © 2010 Trudy Corporation and the Smithsonian Institution, Washington, DC 20560.

Published by Soundprints, an imprint of Trudy Corporation, Norwalk, Connecticut.
www.soundprints.com

All rights reserved. No part of this book may be reproduced or transmitted in any form or
by any means whatsoever without prior written permission of the publisher.

Editor: Laura Gates Galvin
Book Design: Jersey Babcock
Production Coordinator: Chris Dobias
Audio Design: Laura Gates Galvin

First Edition 2010
10 9 8 7 6 5 4 3 2 1
Printed in China

Acknowledgments:
    Soundprints would like to thank Ellen Nanney and Kealy Wilson at the Smithsonian Institution's
Office of Product Development and Licensing for their help in the creation of this book.

*A portion of the publisher's proceeds from your purchase of this licensed product supports the stated educational
mission of the Smithsonian Institution—"the increase and diffusion of knowledge."*

Library of Congress Cataloging-in-Publication Data

Froggy Went a-Courtin' / edited by Laura Gates Galvin ; illustrated by Jacqueline Decker.—1st ed.
    p. cm.—(American favorites)
  Summary: Illustrates the well-known folk song about the courtship and marriage of Froggy and Miss
Mousie. Includes historical note, additional verses, and sheet music.
  ISBN 978-1-60727-009-6 (hardcover)—ISBN 978-1-60727-010-2 (pbk.)
  1. Folk songs, English--Texts. [1. Folk songs.] I. Galvin, Laura Gates, II. Decker, Jacqueline, ill. III.
Frog he would a-wooing go (Folk-song) IV. Title: Froggy went a-courting.
  PZ8.3.F922 2009
  782.42—dc22
  [E]
                                    2008055247

Froggy went a-Courtin'

Edited by Laura Gates Galvin
Illustrated by Jacqueline Decker

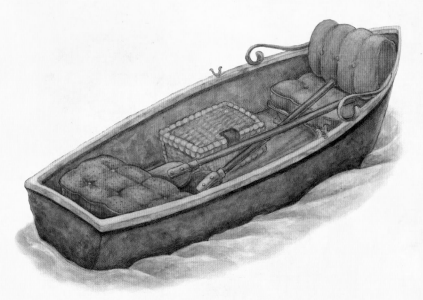

Soundprints®

Where Children Discover...

R0426057079

Froggy went a-courtin' and he did ride,

uh-huh, uh-huh.

Froggy went a-courtin' and he did ride,

uh-huh, uh-huh.

Froggy went a-courtin' and he did ride,

with some flowers by his side,

uh-huh, uh-huh, uh-huh.

He rode up to Miss Mousie's door,
uh-huh, uh-huh.
He rode up to Miss Mousie's door,
uh-huh, uh-huh.
He rode up to Miss Mousie's door,
where he'd often been before,
uh-huh, uh-huh, uh-huh.

Froggy got down on one knee,
uh-huh, uh-huh.
Froggy got down on one knee,
uh-huh, uh-huh.
Froggy got down on one knee,
said, "Miss Mousie, will you marry me?"
Uh-huh, uh-huh, uh-huh.

Where shall the wedding supper be?
Uh-huh, uh-huh.

Where shall the wedding supper be?
Uh-huh, uh-huh.
Where shall the wedding supper be?
Way down yonder in the hollow tree.
Uh-huh, uh-huh, uh-huh.

First to come was a flyin' moth,
uh-huh, uh-huh.
First to come was a flyin' moth,
uh-huh, uh-huh.
First to come was a flyin' moth,
and she spread out the tablecloth,
uh-huh, uh-huh, uh-huh.

Next to come was a bumblebee,
uh-huh, uh-huh.

Next to come was a bumblebee,
uh-huh, uh-huh.

Next to come was a bumblebee,
played the fiddle upon his knee,
uh-huh, uh-huh, uh-huh.

Next to come was a little black flea,
uh-huh, uh-huh.
Next to come was a little black flea,
uh-huh, uh-huh.
Next to come was a little black flea,
danced a jig with a bumblebee,
uh-huh, uh-huh, uh-huh.

Next to come was Mrs. Cow,

uh-huh, uh-huh.

Next to come was Mrs. Cow,

uh-huh, uh-huh.

Next to come was Mrs. Cow,

she tried to dance but she didn't know how,

uh-huh, uh-huh, uh-huh.

Next to come was a hungry snake,
uh-huh, uh-huh.
Next to come was a hungry snake,
uh-huh, uh-huh.

Next to come was a hungry snake,
ate up all the wedding cake,
uh-huh, uh-huh, uh-huh.

Then Froggy and Mousie went off to France,

uh-huh, uh-huh.

Then Froggy and Mousie went off to France,

uh-huh, uh-huh.

Then Froggy and Mousie went off to France

and that's the end of this romance,

uh-huh, uh-huh, uh-huh.

Froggy Went a-Courtin'

Arrangement Copyright 2010 Trudy Corporation

Traditional

Froggy went a-courtin' and he did ride, uh-huh, uh-huh.
Froggy went a-courtin' and he did ride, uh-huh, uh-huh.
Froggy went a-courtin' and he did ride,
with some flowers by his side, uh-huh, uh-huh, uh-huh.

He rode up to Miss Mousie's door, uh-huh, uh-huh.
He rode up to Miss Mousie's door, uh-huh, uh-huh.
He rode up to Miss Mousie's door,
where he'd often been before, uh-huh, uh-huh, uh-huh.

He took Miss Mousie on his knee, uh-huh, uh-huh.
He took Miss Mousie on his knee, uh-huh, uh-huh.
He took Miss Mousie on his knee,
said, "Miss Mousie, will you marry me?" Uh-huh, uh-huh, uh-huh.

"Without my Uncle Rat's consent," uh-huh, uh-huh.
"Without my Uncle Rat's consent," uh-huh, uh-huh.
"Without my Uncle Rat's consent,
I wouldn't marry the President," uh-huh, uh-huh, uh-huh.

Uncle Rat laughed, and he shook his fat sides, uh-huh, uh-huh.
Uncle Rat laughed, and he shook his fat sides, uh-huh, uh-huh.
Uncle Rat laughed, and he shook his fat sides
to think his niece would be a bride, uh-huh, uh-huh, uh-huh.

Where shall the wedding supper be? Uh-huh, uh-huh.
Where shall the wedding supper be? Uh-huh, uh-huh.
Where shall the wedding supper be?
Way down yonder in the hollow tree. Uh-huh, uh-huh, uh-huh.

What shall the wedding supper be? Uh-huh, uh-huh.
What shall the wedding supper be? Uh-huh, uh-huh.
What shall the wedding supper be,
fried mosquito and a black-eyed pea? Uh-huh, uh-huh, uh-huh.

First to come was a flyin' moth, uh-huh, uh-huh.
First to come was a flyin' moth, uh-huh, uh-huh.
First to come was a flyin' moth,
and she spread out the tablecloth, uh-huh, uh-huh, uh-huh.

Next to come was a bumblebee, uh-huh, uh-huh.
Next to come was a bumblebee, uh-huh, uh-huh.
Next to come was a bumblebee,
played the fiddle upon his knee, uh-huh, uh-huh, uh-huh.

Next to come was a little black flea, uh-huh, uh-huh.
Next to come was a little black flea, uh-huh, uh-huh.
Next to come was a little black flea,
danced a jig with a bumblebee, uh-huh, uh-huh, uh-huh.

Next to come was Mrs. Cow, uh-huh, uh-huh.
Next to come was Mrs. Cow, uh-huh, uh-huh.
Next to come was Mrs. Cow,
she tried to dance but she didn't know how, uh-huh, uh-huh, uh-huh.

Next to come was a hungry snake, uh-huh, uh-huh.
Next to come was a hungry snake, uh-huh, uh-huh.
Next to come was a hungry snake,
ate up all the wedding cake, uh-huh, uh-huh, uh-huh.

Then Froggy and Mousie went off to France, uh-huh, uh-huh.
Then Froggy and Mousie went off to France, uh-huh, uh-huh.
Then Froggy and Mousie went off to France,
and that's the end of this romance, uh-huh, uh-huh, uh-huh.

If you want anymore, you can sing it yourself,
uh-huh, uh-huh, uh-huh.

Over the years there have been many different versions and recordings of the ballad, as well as numerous titles. Some of the titles include The Frog's Wooing, Froggy Would a-Wooing Go, There Was a Puggy in a Well, Here's to Cheshire, Here's to Cheese and King Kong Kitchie Kitchie Ki-Me-O.

The first known appearance of the musical version of the song was in 1611 in the Melismata; Musical Phansies Fitting the Court, Citie, and Countrey Humours by English composer Thomas Ravenscroft.

In recent years, popular artists such as Bob Dylan, Elvis Presley and Bruce Springsteen have recorded Froggy Went a-Courtin'.

The English-language folksong, Froggy Went a-Courtin', dates back to at least 1550 when it was published in Wedderburn's Complaynt of Scotland, an important book of Scotland's language. There is also a reference to A Moste Strange Weddinge of the Frogge and the Mouse in the London Company's Register of 1580.